FINDING Mummy's Glow

A story of cancer, family and love

Shine Cancer Support

Shine Cancer Support provides information and support to anyone diagnosed with any cancer in their 20s, 30s and 40s. They offer a mixture of online and in-person events around the UK and also have a well-known podcast, **Not Your Grandma's Cancer Show**. You can find out more at www.shinecancersupport.org.

Published: 2023 by The Book Reality Experience
Leschenault, Western Australia.
ISBN: 978-1-923020-23-8 - Paperback Edition.

To my darling Sam.

Noah adored his Mummy. Her smile was a brilliant torch that made his world shine, and her hugs were warm and comforting.

Noah and his teddy, Mr Snuggles felt the joy of her loving glow.

THE TEDDY BEAR DIARY

But one day, Mummy's glow was not as bright as before. She looked tired and pale. As the days passed, the sunshine that surrounded Noah and Mr Snuggles faded too. Noah sensed that something was wrong.

Mummy told Noah that she had an illness called cancer. She would need medicine to help her get better.

Noah sobbed, "Did I make you sick?"

Mummy gently stroked Noah's cheek.
"Oh, my sweet Noah, you haven't done anything wrong."
Noah wanted to give mummy a cuddle. But would he catch cancer too?

"Cancer is not like a cold," said Mummy.
"You can't catch it. And your cuddles are magical."

Noah tried to understand. He struggled to catch his breath. Was he in a bad dream? Mr Snuggles' soft touch comforted him.

"I want to help Mummy find her glow," Noah said.

Mr Snuggles said they should search for it. Maybe it was hidden in a rainbow! Or a flower! Or a star! If they found Mummy's glow, then her sunshine would dazzle again.

Noah thought this was a great idea, so that afternoon, they began their hunt for Mummy's glow.

Noah and Mr Snuggles looked for anything that sparkled, twinkled or shone.

They looked in the garden, where Mummy liked to plant flowers.

They looked in the kitchen, where Mummy liked to bake cookies.

They looked in the bedroom, where Mummy liked to read books.

But nothing matched Mummy's sparkle.

Everything seemed dull and grey.
Noah began to cry. Would he ever see
Mummy's glow again?

Mr Snuggles whispered, "Don't give up. There is one more possible place that we haven't looked."

Noah wiped his tears. "Where?" he asked.
"Here," said Mr Snuggles, as he pointed to Noah's chest.

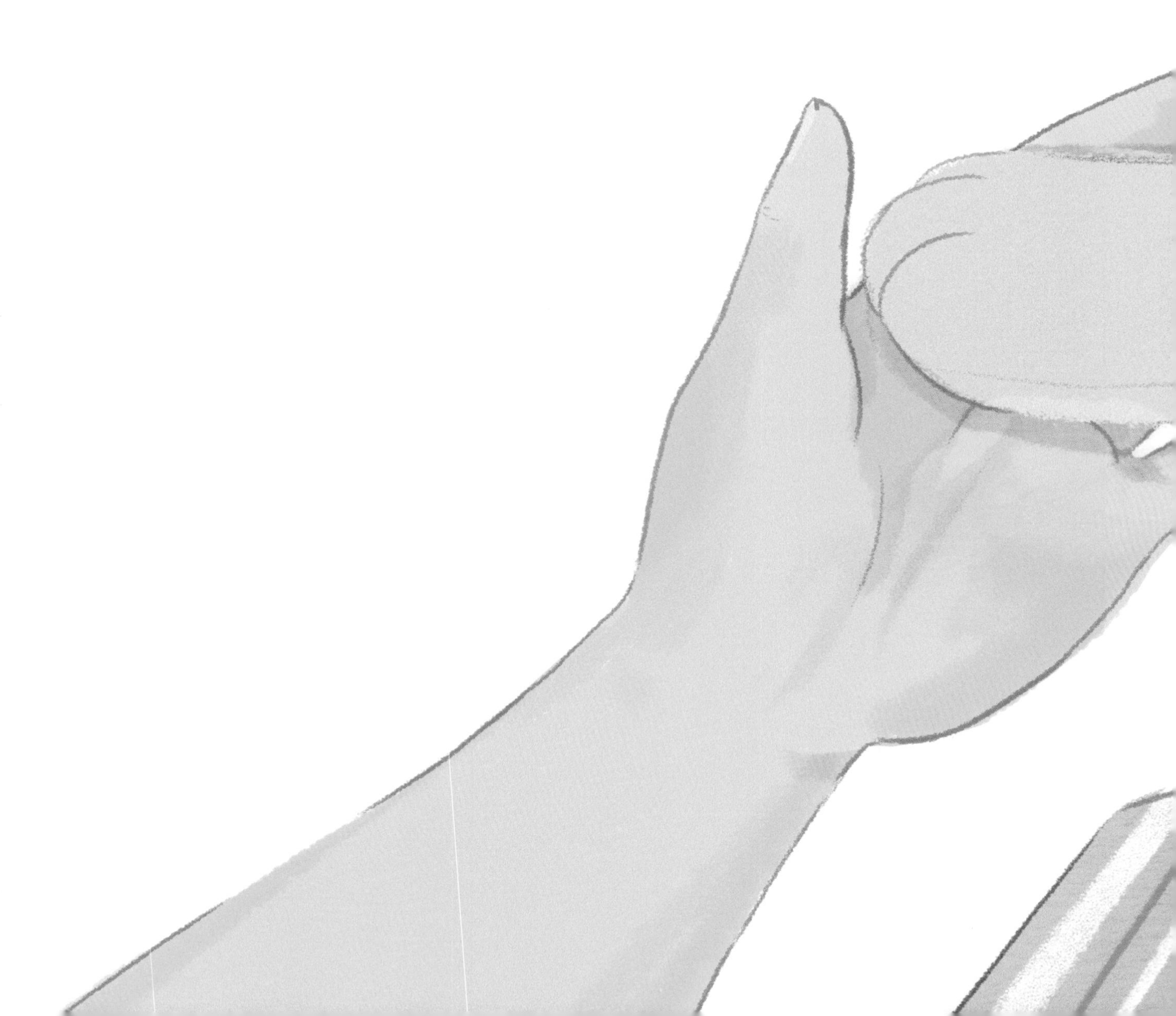

SHINE

Noah closed his eyes and felt deep in his heart. He thought about his mummy's hugs, her stories, her songs and her smile. Soon, a warm and bright sensation filled his heart.

It was like a ray of sunshine. Noah opened his eyes and smiled. Mr Snuggles was right. Noah had found Mummy's glow.

Mummy was resting when Noah found her.
"What did you two do today?" she asked.
"We went on a hunt to find your glow," said Noah.

Mummy smiled. "Did you find it?"
Noah pointed to his heart. "It's right here!"

As Mummy looked at them, her eyes sparkled with love. And Noah and Mr Snuggles cuddled together in the sunshine of her tender smile.

How are you feeling today?

Colour in your emotion that you feel today?

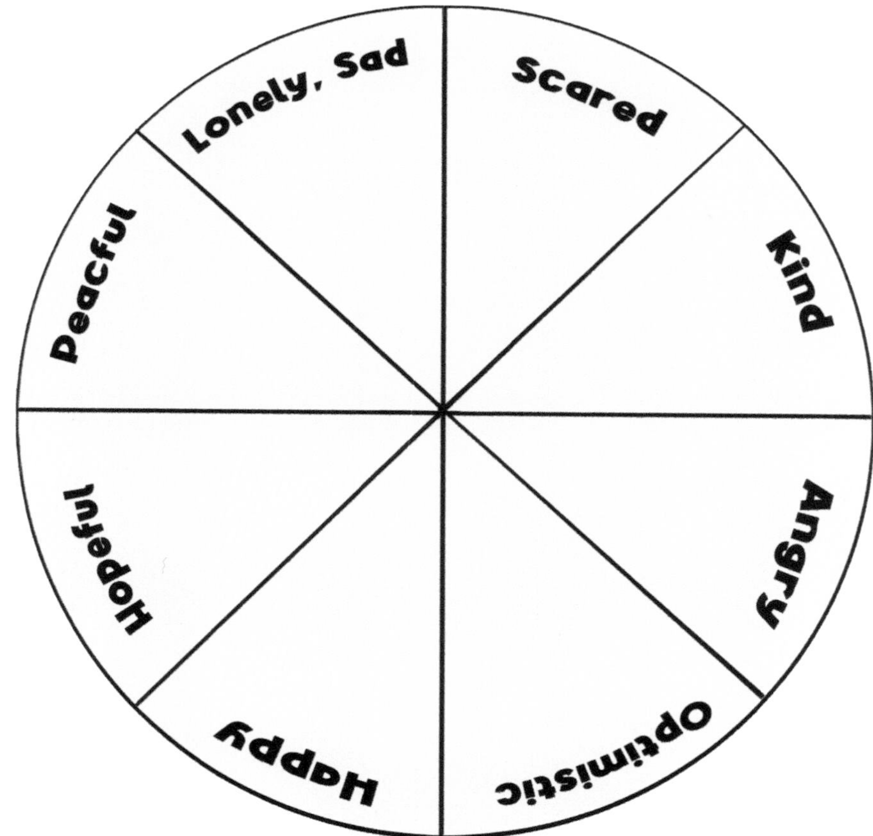

POPPING CANCER BUBBLES

(3 TO 12 YEARS OLD)

Blow bubbles and pretend the bubbles are cancer cells. Let your children pretend to be a chemo shark or a radiation monster. Inspire your children to pop the bubbles to kill the cancer cells. This activity is fun, playful and helps lower your children's stress and worry. Start the activity by blowing bubbles in the air. Your children can pop the bubbles by jumping, slapping, kicking or stomping them. Explain to your children that your chemotherapy or radiation therapy pops your cancer cells just like they pop the bubbles. This activity helps your children understand chemotherapy or radiation therapy.

CREATE A SCRAP BOOK

(6 TO 12 YEARS OLD)

Create a scrap book to bring together great memories and fun times.

In your scrap book you can include pictures of trips, camping, nature walks, your favourite movies or stories. Scrap books are an amazing way to put all your pictures and memories together. Inspire your children to find the materials needed for their scrap book around the house. Get your children to start a collection of things they want in their scrap book. Such things include pictures, seashells, rocks, favourite sayings or quotes from stories or movies.

Creating this scrap book will be an unforgettable experience they will treasure.

Add your solution focused journey:

- You start by identifying your hopes for these present times
- Think about what achieving your hopes would look like
- Think about what you are already doing to move towards your hopes
- Think about what it would look like if you moved just one or two steps closer toward reaching your hopes
- As you go, you learn more about your strengths and what you are capable of.

CREATE A JOURNAL

(ALL AGES)

Write down any thoughts you may have, this can be anything from; stressful thoughts that are playing on your mind, a to do list, your greatest hopes for tomorrow or the future.

Having a journal by your bedside can be very helpful especially if you are having trouble getting to sleep. It can help get rid of negative thoughts and start guiding you toward a more positive mindset, which is why it is important to always finish your last piece of journaling with a list of 3 positive things that went well that day. These can be small things like; I had a shower to big things we got a new car.

BV - #0101 - 181023 - C32 - 254/203/2 - PB - 9781923020238 - Gloss Lamination